Walt Disney's

Pinocchio

Ladybird Books

Geppetto the wood carver lived in a little wooden house with his cat, Figaro, and a goldfish called Cleo. He made lots of marvellous toys, but he had no children to play with them.

One day he made a puppet from some pine wood, and put strings on it so that it could dance. He called the puppet Pinocchio.

When he went to bed that night, Geppetto looked out and saw the bright Evening Star shining in the sky. "Look!" he said to Figaro, "It's a wishing star!"

So Geppetto made a special wish,
*"I wish I may, I wish I might
Have the wish I wish tonight!"*
His secret wish was that little
Pinocchio might become a real
boy!

At that moment the room where Pinocchio lay began to fill with a dazzling bright light. Out of the light stepped the Blue Fairy of the Evening Star, who had heard

Geppetto's secret wish.

The fairy waved her wand over Pinocchio, saying,

"Little puppet made of pine,
Wake! The gift of life is thine!"

Pinocchio sprang to his feet. He could move without strings! And he could talk!

The Blue Fairy told Pinocchio that if he wanted to be a *real* boy, he must first be brave, honest and unselfish.

Now, living in Geppetto's fireplace there was a tiny cricket called Jiminy. The fairy said that Jiminy would be Pinocchio's conscience – the little voice inside us that tells us what is right and what is wrong.

She told Pinocchio that he must *always* listen to Jiminy's advice.

Geppetto was overjoyed, for now Pinocchio was just like a son to him. But one morning, a sly old fox called 'Honest' John Worthington Foulfellow saw Pinocchio going off to school.

‘Honest’ John said to his friend, a down-at-heel cat named Gideon, “We could sell that wooden boy to Stromboli’s Dancing Puppet Show!”

'Honest' John and Gideon told Pinocchio that he could become a rich and famous stage star! All he had to do was to join Stromboli's Marionettes instead of going to school!

“Don’t go, Pinocchio!” said Jiminy Cricket. “Follow your conscience!” But Pinocchio was excited by the thought of an actor’s life, and he would not listen to Jiminy.

Pinocchio danced in the puppet show. He loved all the applause. After the show, he was given a bright gold coin. Pinocchio was delighted.

“Thank you!” he said. “I’m going home now!”

“Home?” said Stromboli. “This is your home!” And he locked Pinocchio in a cage.

That night, the Blue Fairy came again and set Pinocchio free. She asked why Pinocchio hadn't gone straight to school.

Pinocchio told the fairy a terrible lie. "Oh!" he said. "Two monsters with green eyes tied me up. They wanted to chop me into firewood!"

As soon as Pinocchio told the lie, his nose started to grow. Longer and longer it grew. "My nose!" he cried. "What's happening to my nose?"

The Blue Fairy told him that she knew he had been telling a lie. "Like your nose," she said, "a little lie keeps on growing and growing."

Pinocchio promised never to tell a lie again.

Now 'Honest' John and his friend Gideon had spent the evening with a wicked coachman, who said he would pay them to kidnap little boys. In the street afterwards, who should they meet but Pinocchio, running home to Geppetto.

They persuaded Pinocchio he would have more fun if he joined some other boys on the coach.

But Jiminy Cricket, who was Pinocchio's true friend, secretly climbed into the coach as well.

The coach took the noisy party of boys to Pleasure Island. It was like a giant fun fair. All the rides were free, and the boys could be as naughty as they liked.

Pinocchio's new friend was a boy called Lampwick, who was the naughtiest of them all.

But Jiminy Cricket knew that there was something strange about Pleasure Island. He begged Pinocchio to come home, but Pinocchio wanted to stay with Lampwick.

In the end, poor Jiminy decided that he would have to go home alone.

As Jiminy was leaving the island he saw a boat being loaded with crate after crate of donkeys. One of the donkeys was crying, and begging the coachman to let him go home to his mother.

"You boys have had your fun," answered the coachman. "Now you must pay for it!"

Then Jiminy realised that all the silly boys on Pleasure Island were turning into donkeys! He raced off to look for Pinocchio, hoping to find him in time.

But Lampwick was already turning into a donkey! Pinocchio thought it was only a joke. He laughed and laughed!

Then he too started to grow a donkey's tail! His ears became long and hairy! When he saw Jiminy he cried out, "I was stupid to come to this terrible place and behave like a donkey. Please help me!"

Together, Jiminy and Pinocchio escaped from the island. But when they got home the house was dark and empty. Pinocchio sat down on the step. He was sure something bad had happened to his father.

Jiminy and Pinocchio learned from a bird that Geppetto had left home to search for Pinocchio. On the way to the island he and his boat had been swallowed by a mighty whale called Monstro. But Geppetto was still alive inside the whale's belly.

Pinocchio ran to the cliffs with Jiminy and looked down at the ocean. They were both afraid, but they knew that they must rescue Geppetto.

Bravely, they jumped down into the deep water and trudged all over the ocean bed, asking the fish they met where they could find Monstro. But no one knew.

All this time, Monstro was lying asleep. When he woke up he was hungry, so he chased a shoal of fish and gulped them down.

They tumbled into his stomach, where Geppetto managed to hook one to cook for himself.

"My word!" said Geppetto. "It's a heavy one!" He hauled it in.

And clinging to the fish's tail was Pinocchio!

It was clever Pinocchio who thought of a way to escape from Monstro. He stoked up the fire Geppetto had made. It made a lot of smoke, and this made Monstro sneeze. While the whale's mouth was open wide, they paddled their raft out as fast as they could.

But Monstro knew they had got away. As soon as he saw their raft he charged at it. All of them were thrown into the sea – and Geppetto couldn't swim!

Pinocchio swam for mile after mile, struggling to keep his father afloat.

At last they reached the shore, where Jiminy Cricket was waiting for them.

Geppetto was safe! But the effort of saving his father had been too much for brave Pinocchio.

Pinocchio fell to the ground. When Geppetto sat up he found his beloved Pinocchio lying face down in a pool of water.

Geppetto thought that Pinocchio was dead.

Geppetto cried as he carried his little boy home and laid him on the bed. Then the dazzling light filled the room again, and out of it came the voice of the Blue Fairy saying,

"Awake, Pinocchio, awake!"

Pinocchio had truly proved he was brave, honest and unselfish. Now the Blue Fairy kept her word, and gave Pinocchio his life. But this time he was a *real* boy, not one made out of wood.

What a party they all had to celebrate! It was like Christmas! Jiminy sat on the windowsill and watched them. Then he looked up at the Evening Star. "Thank you, Blue Fairy!" he said quietly.

For now that Pinocchio was a real boy, he had his own voice of conscience.

Jiminy's work was finished.